SHOWDOWN

GRIDIRON

SHOWDOWN

K.R. COLEMAN

darbycreek

MINNEAPOLIS

Darby Creek
A division of Lerner Publishing Group, Inc.
241 First Avenue North
Minneapolis, MN 55401 USA

For reading levels and more information, look up this title at
www.lernerbooks.com.

Cover and interior images: © Eky Studio/Shutterstock.com (metal bolts); © Kriangsak Osvapoositkul/Shutterstock.com (rust texture); © pattern line/Shutterstock.com (scratched texture); © Eugene Onischenko/Dreamstime.com (stadium); © Vladimir Mucibabic/Shutterstock.com (players).

Main body text set in Janson Text LT Std 12/17.5.
Typeface provided by Adobe Systems.

Library of Congress Cataloging-in-Publication Data

The Cataloging-in-Publication Data for *Showdown* is on file at the Library of Congress.
ISBN 978-1-5124-3978-6 (lib. bdg.)
ISBN 978-1-5124-5354-6 (pbk.)
ISBN 978-1-5124-4867-2 (EB pdf)

Manufactured in the United States of America
1-42227-25776-2/20/2017

This book is dedicated to Landon, number 50. A heroic young man loved by so many. A kid who could make others smile.

It's two in the morning and I'm riding in the back of a pickup truck with my best friend, Walter. He pulls the strings on his hoodie tighter, trying to brace against the cold. I pull my black knit hat down low over my ears and cross my arms. I wish I would've dressed warmer, but at football practice the past few days, I've been plenty warm.

The three guys up front—all seniors and top players on our team—are nice and warm. I can hear them talking and laughing through a small window that slides open between us. Neko, our team captain, is driving, and Jason and Cam are cracking jokes. One of them cranked up the music so that it's blasting loudly into the night, but when we cross the highway and enter into the town of Winfield, I hear Neko tell them to turn it off. Everyone is quiet now.

"Why couldn't they be this quiet when they pulled up to my house?" I whisper to Walter, but he just shrugs as he pulls out a mini candy bar from the pocket of his sweatshirt.

When Neko showed up at my house, he revved his truck's engine just as I climbed out my first-floor bedroom window and dropped to the ground. The other guys started laughing and talking so loudly I thought for sure they would wake up Gram. She doesn't sleep all that well as it is. As we drove away, I expected a light to go on in her room, but it didn't.

"Hey, Gibby," Neko says to me through the window. "You glad you decided to stop being a baby and sneak out with us?"

"Not really," I mumble under my breath, annoyed, as I look at the dark road.

My real name is Tobias James Gibson, and everyone used to call me Toby until I made the varsity football team this year. Now Neko has everyone calling me Gibby, and I hate the name. I wish he'd just call me by my number like he does with the other players who don't get a lot of playing time.

Walter rolls his eyes at Neko's nickname for me and pulls another little chocolate bar out of his pocket. He's like a human vending machine lately. He's been constantly eating, probably because he's grown at least three inches since the start of football this summer. His mother has had to buy him two new pairs of cleats this season.

"I don't even know why they invited us along," Walter says, shoving the second piece of candy into his mouth.

Most of the guys on this mission are upperclassman. Walter and I are the only sophomores, and we've spent most of the season on the bench. I'm the backup quarterback, and Walter is a backup receiver. We've played a combined total of seventeen minutes this season—only getting our chance on the field when our team is way ahead. Last year, on JV, we both played every game.

Next year, Coach has told us, and I don't blame him. This year's seniors are fast and unstoppable. They're the reason we're going to the state championship next week. I hope we can be as good without them next year.

Neko makes a sharp right. Walter smashes into me as we turn into a fancy Winfield neighborhood. As we try to push ourselves back to a normal sitting position, Neko slows the truck and the headlights go dark. The only sound is the tires rolling across the pavement. We make our way past homes that look like they could be on the cover of a magazine. Some have attached garages bigger than the entire first floor of Gram's house. The lawns are all wide and neat. Everyone seems to have raked up all their leaves (or maybe hired someone to do it for them), something I promised I'd do for my Gram but haven't gotten around to yet.

Neko slows down and parks next to a sprawling park.

"Check that out," Walter says, pointing to a playground. There are six slides, a climbing wall, bridges, and a zip line. And behind that are tennis courts, two basketball courts, and some soccer fields. It's way nicer than any of the parks back in Edison.

Walter jumps out of the back of the truck and heads right to the playground.

"Where are you going?" Neko hisses.

"I just want to check it out," Walter says, looking longingly at the park.

"We didn't come here to play. We came here for revenge," Neko says, nodding toward the cluster of trees at the edge of the park. On the other side of the small woods is Winfield High.

Chapter 2

Yesterday we arrived at school to discover thousands of plastic forks stabbed into our football field in the shape of a giant W for Winfield and rotten eggs smashed all over our bleachers.

The Winfield Wildcats are our biggest rivals. Our schools are just a few miles apart. A highway runs between our two towns—a division that runs just as deep. They're the only team we lost to this year and will be our opponents at the state tournament.

Coach Wilcox made our team clean everything up. We spent almost the whole practice pulling up forks and hosing down the bleachers. That was time we should have spent practicing for the big game. But Neko must have used the break from running plays to think, because after practice he texted a bunch of us to gather at an empty field on the edge of town. When we met there, he laid out his plan for revenge, and everyone agreed to carry it out tonight.

An old beat-up minivan, two more cars, and another truck pull up. A dozen other guys all pile out. Big guys. Tall guys. I feel like a little kid. Even Walter towers above me these days.

I wish his growth spurt would rub off on me, especially at times like these. I'm barely five foot nine, but at least I'm barrel-chested— built like my father, my mom has told me. She has shown me pictures of him when he was eighteen, but I don't remember him. He took off a year after I was born.

As we all gather around Neko, I'm jostled by a couple of the guys who are goofing around. They act like they don't even see me standing there.

"Shhhh," Neko says as he glares at the guys who are talking. "You want to get caught?"

He signals everyone to gather around him like we do before a game.

"Everyone armed?" he asks.

We all pull cans of chocolate frosting out of pockets and plastic bags.

"This is war," Neko says, opening up his can of frosting and smearing two lines of frosting across each cheek. Then he passes the tub around our circle. We all smear two lines across our faces. "We get in. We get out. We don't get caught."

Neko marches across the soccer field and toward the woods. We all follow. Frost covers the ground and the blades of grass crunch beneath our feet.

When we get to the woods, Neko turns on a flashlight and enters the dark woods first. I didn't think to grab a flashlight, but a few of the other guys did. I try to follow their lights, but everyone is moving too fast. I trip over a log and crash into a huge guy in front of me. He's so big that I just bounce off him and hit the ground.

"Watch it," he snarls. A few of the guys behind me laugh. I want to be treated like a part of the team, but I'm starting to wonder if all of this is worth it.

We start to climb a steep hill. Suddenly there's a loud snap of a tree branch from somewhere deep in the woods.

We all freeze. My heart is pounding hard. Before she left for deployment, I promised my mom that I would be good for Gram—take care of her and not cause her trouble. If I get caught out here in the middle of the night, I would definitely get in trouble. And Gram doesn't need to worry about me *and* Mom.

Neko shines a light in the direction of the sound, but there are only trees and darkness. I feel like I can hardly breathe.

"Keep going," Neko says after a moment. "It's probably just a raccoon or something."

I don't know if I believe him, but we all scurry up the steep, muddy hill. Soon we step out of the woods and onto a sprawling lawn.

Winfield High stands in front of us. It's a newly built school with a three-story glass lobby in the front. It sits on top of the hill like a glass castle and looks like it might actually be as *expensive* as a castle.

As we approach the lobby, Neko turns and says, "Uncap now."

We open up the canisters of frosting and pull back the tinfoil covering as we head toward the windows.

"Work fast," Neko orders.

Walter and I head to the far end of the lobby and begin to spread frosting. There are a few lights on inside the school. I can see leather couches set up around a gas fireplace.

At the other end of the lobby is a small coffee stand. A silver espresso machine sits on a counter. "Walter," I say, pointing a frosted finger, "they have their own coffee shop."

Neko comes up behinds us and I jump. He glares at us and says, "Less talking, more frosting."

I spread another handful of frosting and watch as Neko, Cam, and Jason saunter to the front doors. Neko takes the lid off another canister, dips a rubber scraper into it, and in large, frosted letters writes: CAKE EATERS.

"What does that even mean?" Walter nods at the frosted words.

"I don't know. That they're rich? That they can eat cake every day for breakfast if they want?"

"I'd eat cake every day for breakfast," Walter says.

"I know you would," I laugh. Walter would probably eat an entire cake at any time of day if someone set one in front of him.

My canister of frosting is nearly empty when Zander, our team's star wide receiver, comes charging out of his lookout position near the entrance to the school's parking lot and yells: "Cops!"

"Retreat," Neko yells. "Everybody retreat!"

Still holding a canister of frosting, I run with the rest of my teammates toward the woods. We slip and slide down the hill, tripping over branches. I bump against some of the other guys, bouncing between them, but nobody says anything. No one dares turn on a flashlight. Finally, we find our way out of the woods and run across one of the soccer fields toward the cars where everyone is gathered.

"Drive slow and cool. Don't speed. And don't follow each other," Neko tells the others as Walter and I hop in the back of his truck and Cam and Jason scramble into the front seat.

Neko lets all the other cars go first, and then he drives slowly out of the neighborhood. The car in front of us turns right, so we turn left on a road that leads down to Lake Washington.

"Can I have that?" Walter points to the can of frosting still in my hand. I hand it to him. He pulls out a bag of chips, dips one chip into the frosting, and eats it.

"I should sell these. Frosted potato chips." He dips another chip into the frosting, but it breaks apart. He digs it out and hands it to me. "Try it."

I shake my head. My stomach feels sick. Behind us, I see a cop car heading over a hill on the road. Lights flashing. Siren on.

Chapter 3

"Cops," I say through the open window between the bed of the truck and the cab.

"Get down," Neko whispers to us.

Walter and I lie flat, and I pull a tarp over the both of us. Even though I haven't taken driver's ed yet, I know it's illegal to ride around in the back of a pickup truck like this—not to mention vandalize a school.

Neko pulls over. The truck comes to a stop. My heart is beating fast. I can smell the sugary frosting still on my face and it makes me feel sick. I think about how angry Gram will be if she gets a call from the police.

The sirens grow louder. *What is Neko going to say?* I wonder. *How is he going to explain why he, Cam, and Jason are out this late at night? What if the cop finds Walter and me?*

Peering out from under the tarp, I can see the flashing red light growing brighter and brighter, and then the sound of the siren passes us. It fades away down the road.

Neko waits a few seconds and then pulls back on the road. I let out the breath I've been holding in, and the guys up front start laughing and slapping each other on the back.

I sit up and peer through the sliding window.

Neko is gripping the wheel.

"Let's head home," I say.

"Not yet," Neko says. "We aren't done."

I look at Walter.

"Where are we going?" he asks.

"I have no idea," I reply.

We drive along the shore of Lake Washington, past a yacht club and little boutiques where I know everything must cost a fortune. When we cross over a small bridge,

Neko slows down and pulls off onto a small gravel lot.

Neko and the guys up front get out of the truck. I take out my phone and look at the time: 4:15 a.m. I need to get back home. My Gram gets up around 5:00 every morning. It's a habit she can't break even though she's retired now. She used to work as the head cook at the cafeteria at my high school. Teachers are always asking about her, which means that even now that she's retired, my Gram knows basically everything that happens at the school—especially when I get in trouble.

"What are we doing?" I ask as Walter pours the last of the potato chip crumbs into his mouth.

"Lars Bristol lives there," Neko says, leaning against the truck and pointing to a huge white house sitting on a hill overlooking the bay. "That red BMW parked out front is his, and I have a couple of extra cans of frosting I don't want to go to waste."

Lars is the quarterback and team captain for the Wildcats. Rumor has it he's being recruited by a bunch of Division I schools, something that drives Neko crazy because he's convinced Lars isn't all that good. He insists that the only reason recruiters have even paid attention is because Lars's dad hired a PR firm to represent him.

I look down at my phone again. I need to get back home.

"I don't know," I say.

Neko shakes his head and looks over at Cam and Jason.

"You believe this kid?" he says. "We invite him along, and he acts all scared." He turns back to me with a serious look on his face. "Look, you're here because you're supposed to be good. I thought you were going to lead the team next year. We don't need a coward for a quarterback."

I put my phone back in my pocket and stand up in the back of the truck. I'm not going to let Neko think I'm the weak link on the team.

"Fine," I say, jumping out of the truck bed and landing on the gravel with a thud. "Let's get it done."

Neko hands me a can of frosting and I wait for him to lead the way, but he just continues to lean against the truck.

"Hurry up," he says.

"You're not going?" I ask.

"Nah," he says. "It's my job to get you ready for next year. Build up your courage. Push you. Coach thinks you have potential to be the starting quarterback next year, but I told him I didn't think you had the confidence or strength. Prove me wrong."

I look at him, angry that he said something like that to Coach. Neko doesn't know me. He's never seen me really play. Last year, while playing JV, I not only threw the ball for touchdowns, but also ran it down the field, stiff-arming defenders along the way.

I head to the house and hear footsteps behind me.

"I'm coming too," Walter whispers.

"That's what I like to see—team players!" Neko yells as we walk along the shoulder of the road and turn up a long, steep driveway. I wish he would just shut up—he's going to wake up Lars or his parents, and then we are going to get in real trouble.

As we get near the car, a dog barks somewhere in the house. A deep bark. We both freeze.

"That dog sounds mean," Walter says.

"Then let's hurry," I say. We run to the car and spread some frosting on the windows with our bare hands. As I spread some on the driver's window, the car alarm goes off.

The lights flash. The horn honks. *Whoot! Whoot! Whoot!* One of the house's flood lights goes on. The front door opens up, and the dog we heard barking comes flying out the front door. It looks as if it's half wolf and half bear.

"Run!" I yell at Walter.

Walter and I bolt. We both drop the frosting—which turns out to be a good thing because it distracts the dog, who stops to lick the container while Walter and I get away. We sprint down the driveway and back to the truck.

"Big dog!" I yell. "Big, big dog!"

"Now that's some good hustle," Neko says,

laughing. "Get in!"

We jump in the truck bed, and Neko squeals back on the road. I look back to see the dog just behind us at the end of the driveway. Teeth flashing. Eyes glaring. Cam and Jason turn around in their seat barking at us like dogs, then turn back around and start to laugh again.

My heart is racing, and Walter's eyes are still huge.

"That thing was a beast," Walter says.

"We're lucky we weren't mauled," I agree, and we sit in silence for the rest of the ride.

I've never been so happy to see Gram's house. I hop out of the truck and look at my phone. It's five o'clock on the dot. As I head to the side of the house, I see the light in my grandmother's room flick on. I hurry to my window and boost myself up. I shimmy through my window, kick off my shoes, and hop into my bed just as I hear Gram's footsteps head down the hall. She pauses outside my room but then continues to the kitchen, where I hear her making coffee.

Chapter 4

I drift off to sleep, only to wake up forty-five minutes later to the smell of baking apples and the sound of my Gram's voice.

She's a tiny woman and reminds me of a bird with her puffy, silver hair, her skinny legs, and the bright blue sweater that she always wears around the house.

"Tobias James," she says, standing over my bed. "Your alarm has been going off for ten minutes now. Time to get up." She opens the curtains.

Light streams in. It hurts my eyes and my head. I feel sick. My body and brain just want to sleep.

Gram hands me my phone. It's still beeping. I turn it off.

"What's that on your face?" she asks me as I sit up in my bed.

I touch my cheek.

"Uh, frosting," I say. I can't think of a lie fast enough.

"Why do you have frosting all over your face?"

This time I'm more prepared. "It's, uhh, for zits. I read somewhere it clear ups your skin."

Gram looks at me, squints her hazel eyes, and then shakes her head.

"Why would you believe such a thing? Frosting is all oil and sugar and who knows what else, especially if it comes out of one of those nasty cans."

"I read it on the internet."

"That doesn't make it true." Gram rolls her eyes and turns back toward the door. "Question things," she tells me over her shoulder as she leaves my room. "Research."

As I get out of bed, I notice that my clothes have frosting on them too. I take them off, fold them into a ball, and hide them under my bed. Even my pillow case has brown smudges across it. I rip that off and tuck it under the bed with my clothes. I'll have to wash them on my own so Gram doesn't see them like this. For now I hide my pillow under my blankets so Gram doesn't notice the missing pillowcase.

I hurry to the shower, and as the warm water washes over me, I feel bad for lying to Gram. I feel bad for sneaking out. I think back to the promise I made to my mom before she was deployed.

I know Gram would've been worried if she found out I was gone, and I know that my mom would be disappointed in me if she found out what I was up to last night. More than anything, I need my mom to stay strong and focused over there. She's got bigger things to worry about.

When I enter the kitchen, I see that Gram has already baked four pies and is starting on a casserole. She bakes for the church and the whole neighborhood, delivering food to anyone who's sick or going through hard times.

"Come here," Gram says as I'm about to head out the door. She never lets me leave without a hug. She smells of freshly baked bread and the rosemary she was chopping near the stove, and I try to remember how my mom smells—the scent of the shampoo she always uses—but I've begun to forget. It's been four months since she left and over a week since I've heard her voice.

Gram seems to know I'm thinking about my mom and hugs me a bit tighter.

"She's going to call soon," she says. "Sometime this week, I'm sure."

And I nod at this. My mom can't always call, but this has been the longest we've gone without hearing from her.

Chapter 5

Walter and I always meet up outside a gas station a few blocks away from our houses and walk to school together. When I get there, he's holding a box of snack cakes.

"Cake eater," he says with a smile as he offers me one.

"Thanks," I say. Gram never allows food like this in her house. If she wanted cake, she'd make a cake from scratch. Sifting the flour, whipping the frosting—everything.

As Walter and I start walking to school, Neko drives by, honks his horn, and pulls over.

"Want some cake?" Walter holds up the box.

Neko laughs and holds out his hand. Walter tosses him a wrapped-up snack cake.

"Get in," Neko says pointing to the passenger door.

"Front seat this time," Walter says to me as we walk around the truck and slide into the cab.

It'll be a big deal to show up to school with Neko. He's got a specific spot in the parking lot. Nothing official from the school says it's his, but no one else ever dares to park in it. A crowd of players and friends linger there in the mornings waiting for him to arrive.

"That was a great night!" Neko says.

"Wish I could see their faces this morning," Walter laughs.

"Yeah," Neko says, tapping his thumbs against the steering wheel. He's quiet for a moment and then he looks over at us and says, "Let's drive there. Right now. Let's go check it out."

"You're never supposed to return to the scene of a crime," I say, looking at the clock on the dashboard. I don't want to be late to school. I have a Spanish quiz first hour.

"No crime committed," Neko says. "Just a little prank, and we've got time."

I don't know what clock he's looking at, but I know there is no way we'll make it to Winfield and back in ten minutes. I look over at Walter, but he just shrugs at me and finishes off another snack cake. Neko does a sudden U-turn just before we get to our school parking lot.

I look back at the building as we drive away from Edison High. I think about how it looks nothing like Winfield High. Our school was built back in the seventies. It's a long, rambling building with a flat roof that leaks when the snow melts in the spring. And we definitely don't have a glass lobby—just small, narrow windows with a view of the dammed-up river that powers the Edison Hydropower Plant. That's why our team is called the Eddies and our mascot is a lightning bolt. It's all pretty lame.

We cross over the highway and head into Winfield. We drive through the same neighborhood where we were last night, but this time we don't pull into the parking lot by the park. Instead, Neko turns down a road that leads to the school. I expect him to just drive down the road, but he turns right into the school's parking lot and drives up to the very front of the school.

Winfield's parking lot is filled with shiny, expensive cars. As we get closer to the school, we see a crowd gathered out front. We slow down and idle right in front of the school. A custodian is spraying the windows with a hose. Frosting slides down the glass. Brown chocolate puddles stain the white sidewalk.

I see a bunch of football players in their letter jackets, standing off to one side. They're big, meaty guys, and they look mad.

Neko honks his horn and tells us to roll the window down on our side.

"The Eddies are going to kick your butt!" he shouts at the players.

The expressions on the Winfield players' faces harden when they realize who we are. Two of them run toward the truck, and another one launches a coffee cup. It goes right through the open window and splashes all over the dash and windshield. We're lucky the cup was almost empty—the coffee is barely lukewarm.

As the football players chase after us, Neko squeals his tires, racing out of the parking lot and onto the road.

"Wipe it up!" Neko points to the dashboard and windshield.

Walter and I look around for a towel or paper towels or even a kleenex, but there isn't anything.

"Use your sleeves," Neko says.

Walter and I look at each other. I'm wearing a light gray US ARMY sweatshirt my mom got me before she left. I'm not going to use my sleeve, so I tear a couple of pieces of paper out of a notebook in my backpack and use them to soak up the mess.

"You're just smearing it around," Neko shouts. "Use your sleeves!"

"No!" I yell back.

It's the first time I've ever stood up to Neko, and he looks over at me like he wants to slug me. But I'm not going to back down about this. Just as things are probably going to get nasty, Walter pulls a wad of napkins out of his backpack and wipes up the mess.

Neko blasts through one yellow light after another. I keep looking in the side mirror for cops as he speeds across the highway and into Edison, but nobody catches us. *He's lucky again*, I think, when we drive into the school's parking lot.

No one is outside. By the time we enter the building, the second bell has rung and everyone is already in class. We're ten minutes late.

"Put it on my tab," Neko says with a smile as he saunters past Mrs. Murray, the woman at the front desk. Mrs. Murray doesn't smile back. Instead, she holds up a hand, makes him stop, and gives him a pink detention slip.

"That's three tardies in three days," she says. "I'll see you after school."

"I can't do detention." He leans against her desk. "I'm not sure if you've heard, but we're going to state and the team needs me at practice today."

"You can study your playbook in detention," Mrs. Murray says. "I'll make sure your coach knows where you are."

***

When I get to class, my teacher is already collecting the Spanish quiz.

I hand her the slip.

"Unexcused," she says, raising an eyebrow. "Can't let you make up the quiz."

"Really?" I ask, half surprised, half pleading.

"Really," she says. "Be on time."

I slump down at my desk and pretend to pay attention to the conjugation of verbs. But I'm mostly just staring at the whiteboard, trying hard not to let my eyes close.

Chapter 6

After school, I meet Walter at the side doors. He's chugging a soda.

"So tired," he says.

"Me too," I agree.

He opens his backpack and hands me a can. I drink it.

"Hey, Toby, Walter, heard you got Lars's car good," a senior from our team says as we head to the locker room. "Nice job."

I nod at this and Walter grins. I don't know what else to do. Usually the upperclassmen act like they don't even know our names.

A couple more guys give us the nod, and

for the first time this entire year, I feel like a part of the team. I figure the prank wasn't all that bad. We didn't do any real damage.

In the locker room, Coach Wilcox comes out of his office and says, "I want you all dressed and out on the field in five." His jaw is clenched. Most of the time Coach is a positive guy, but not today. I wonder if he has heard about what we did last night.

"Move it!" He shouts and then slams his office door. Yeah, I'm guessing he knows.

We hurry into our uniforms. Just as I pull my jersey on, I see Neko saunter into the locker room. I'm not sure how he got out of detention, but that's typical Neko.

Some of the guys high-five him, and Jason tells him what Coach just said. But Neko takes his time and is the last one to arrive out on the field.

"Take a knee," Coach says, pacing in front of us. "Got a call from the principal of Winfield High early this morning." He pauses and just lets the moment hang there. "It sounds likes some guys from this team made a mess at their school."

A couple of the seniors laugh, and I know by Coach's face that it was a mistake.

"You and you," he points to the guys. "Give me twenty. Now."

The two huge lineman move to the side and start doing pushups. I look down at my hands. I still have frosting under a few of my nails.

"The Wildcats deserved it," Neko says. "They started this whole thing."

"Enough," Coach says. "No more pranks. Got it? These things can get out of control. Put an end to it. Now! The best revenge is to work hard and beat them at state. Have I made myself clear?"

We nod.

"Look at me," he says and then waits for all of us to look up at him. "Did you hear what I just told every one of you?"

"Yes," we all mumble.

"Louder," Coach says. "I couldn't hear you."

"Yes, sir!" we all yell back.

"No more pranks. Focus on state."

Coach blows his whistle and orders us to

run laps.

After my first lap around the field, Coach calls me over. I think I'm going to get in some kind of trouble, but instead he hands me a red jersey. "You'll be taking Neko's place at practice today."

Then he calls Neko over. I keep my head down as I jog out onto the field. Behind me, I can hear Coach yelling at Neko for skipping detention and being disrespectful to Mrs. Murray. He sends him over to the stands to run the stairs.

Coach blows his whistle and we all gather around.

He sets up a scrimmage and tells everyone I'll be playing quarterback.

We hit the field and run play after play.

It feels strange to have the older guys huddle around me, and I'm glad I've spent so much time studying the playbook.

I'm playing with the starters, and these guys are a machine. They run each play with precision and speed. When I throw, there is a receiver there waiting to catch the pass. When

I hand off, no one fumbles the ball. Everyone is focused, and no one makes a mistake.

After a few plays, Coach calls Zander over to work with special teams, and Walter takes his place as wide receiver. The first play Walter's nervous and drops the ball. The other guys give him a hard time, but when we run the play again, he catches the ball and runs it in for a touchdown.

I see Coach watching us.

"Nice job," Coach yells, nodding at Walter. "But Gibson, you've got to keep moving your feet. Move faster. A quicker release."

I nod at this and push myself to act faster, but when I do, I overthrow the ball. Walter is able to make up for this with his long arms. It's like he's made of elastic out there, reaching and catching balls thrown too high or too wide. He's making me look good, even though I know my aim is off.

Near the end of practice I step back to throw one last pass, when suddenly I'm hit and taken down by Cam Jensen, one of our best defenders. I saw him barreling toward me, but

I didn't think he'd knock me to the ground.

I slowly get up and look around. Coach's back is to us. He's working with Zander. He didn't see a thing.

"What are you doing?" Walter yells at Cam. He walks up to Cam and pushes him in the chest. "He's wearing a red jersey. You don't hit the guy wearing a red jersey."

Cam pushes Walter back. They're the same height, but Cam has at least eighty pounds on Walter, and Walter stumbles backward.

"He waited too long," Cam says getting in Walter's face. "You wait too long, you get sacked. I was teaching him a lesson. Now I'm teaching you one. Don't tell me what to do."

"What's going on?" Coach asks as he walks toward us.

"We're good," Cam says, raising his hands up in the air and looking at me as if to say, *Keep your mouth shut.* When I look over at the bleachers, I see Neko nodding at Cam.

As we head back to the locker room at the end of practice, Neko comes up behind me and says, "Gibby, my boy, you have to move faster out there. You think too much, wait too long. Do that and you'll get a smackdown."

I hear Cam laugh at this. He's behind me too, but I refuse to turn around.

In the locker room, I hurry to get undressed. I'm covered in sweat and mud. I wrap a towel around my waist and head to the showers.

Just as I'm about to turn the corner into the showers, one of our linebackers—a 240-pound, six-foot-four guy—runs past me, barely holding onto his towel, yelling, "Skunk!"

"What?" My question echoes off the locker room walls around me.

When I look into the shower room, there isn't just one skunk, there are three. They all look scared and trapped, and their tails are raised.

I slowly back away and realize the skunks are following me.

We all run outside. Some guys are holding towels around their waists; some guys are half-undressed. Neko is standing there in a pair of tighty-whities and nothing else.

Suddenly there is a flashing of light. Three people I don't recognize are holding up phones and taking pictures. Then they jump into a car that is idling just a few feet away.

On the sidewalk outside our locker room, written in white chalk are the words: The Eddies Stink.

"No!" Neko yells. "No way!"

Coach comes running out the door after us. One of the skunks follows him out the door.

Everyone backs away.

"Hold the door open," I yell. "The other skunks will follow."

But no one goes near the door. So with one hand still firmly holding onto my towel, I open the door, and sure enough, the other two skunks scamper out.

The three skunks head down a small hill and across a field—straight toward the Edison Hydropower Plant that rises behind our school like a metal spider.

"Well," Coach says, looking down at the sidewalk, "I guess Winfield's coach didn't give his guys the same talk." And then he looks at us all standing there shivering in the cold night air and says, "There will be no revenge, except for beating them at state next week. You will not retaliate. Am I clear?"

"Yeah," we mumble. Neko is standing next to me, but says nothing. He's staring off to the place where the skunks disappeared.

"Woooheee, it reeks in here. Plug your noses, boys," Cam says as we head back into the locker room.

The skunks sprayed all over our locker room. We dress as fast as we can and head out, but we can't get away from the smell of skunk. It's all over us.

Halfway home, Walter's phone starts buzzing.

"Oh no," he says, looking at a text.

"What?" I ask.

He shows me a video of Neko in his underwear, hopping around and plugging his nose. Behind Neko is the rest of our team, all yelling and running around as if a bomb had gone off. There's me in my towel looking skinny, and Walter yanking up his pants.

The Eddies Stink reads the caption beneath

the video. Then I notice the number of views, and my stomach drops. This thing has gone viral. The comment section is filling up as we watch the number of views grow.

As we watch, a message from Neko pops up on Walter's phone telling us to meet at Lou's Pizza Pit in an hour.

I head home, and the first thing Gram says when I walk in the house is, "Why do you smell like skunk?"

I tell her about the surprise we all discovered in the shower after practice. She plugs her nose and laughs before ordering me to throw my clothes in the wash.

After I've showered and changed, I explain that we have a team meeting at Pizza Pit.

"Hmm," she says, looking at me as if she knows that something is up. I can tell she's thinking twice about letting me go.

"We're just getting together to talk game

strategy," I say.

"Well, eat something good for you before you leave." Gram makes me sit down and eat a bowl of the soup she's been simmering on the stove.

Through the kitchen window I see Walter bike up the driveway. Gram sees him too and raps on the glass, motioning for him to come inside.

Walter drops his bike and hurries to the door. Gram has a bowl of soup waiting for him at the table, and he's in the chair before I can even say hello. Walter loves Gram's cooking and eats two bowls of soup before I even finish one.

"That's the best soup I've ever had," he flatters Gram as we clear our plates.

"Thank you," she says with a smile as we head out the door. "Nothing better than feeding growing boys."

We bike to the strip mall a few blocks away. Half the stores are empty now. Over in Winfield, they built a nicer, three-story mall. No one shops here anymore.

At Pizza Pit, Walter orders a large pizza as soon as we sit down with team.

"How can you still be hungry?" I ask.

"I just am," he says.

Neko holds up his phone, which is playing the same video Walter and I watched earlier, and says, "We're getting them back."

"How?" Cam asks.

"That's why you are all here," Neko says.

"What they did was pretty good," Jason says, smiling. "I mean, how did they get those skunks into our locker room without being sprayed? Seriously. They win."

Neko glares at him and says, "We haven't even started. Now all of you"—he looks at everyone sitting around the table—"give me your best idea."

"Pigs," Cam blurts. "Let's set some pigs loose in their locker room."

"Or chickens," someone else says.

"My uncle has a farm not far from here," Walter says. "But he just raises cows and organic vegetables."

"Does he have one of those mean bulls?"

someone asks.

"I don't think so," Walter says, shaking his head. "All the cows are pretty nice. They all have names like Star and Toffee and Milky Way."

I look at Walter like he's crazy for even bringing this up.

"We can't just go around stealing animals," Neko says. I nod at this. The guy is more reasonable than I thought. "But . . ." Neko puts his hand on Walter's shoulder.

"Where there are cows, there's cow poop," Neko says. "We fill up a bunch of bags and spread it all over the field."

"Manure," Walter corrects. "That's what my uncle calls it—manure."

Neko looks at him and says, "I think your uncle wouldn't even notice or care if we filled up a few Hefty bags."

"Let's do it!" some guys shout.

A couple of guys shake their head.

"Coach will blow a gasket," Zander says. "I'm out."

"Come on," Neko pleads.

But Zander just picks up his cup of soda, takes a last sip, and walks out. A couple more guys follow. I kick Walter under the table. I want us to leave too, but Walter doesn't move.

"Tonight," Neko says, looking around at everyone who stayed behind. "We head to Walter's uncle's farm. I'll bring the garbage bags. You bring shovels!"

Neko beams at Walter and says, "Text everyone the address, and we'll meet there at midnight." And then he turns to the dozen or so guys left sitting around the table.

"Who stinks?" Neko asks with a grin.

"The Wildcats!" Cam shouts, pounding the table with his fist. All I can think is that this isn't going to end well.

Chapter 8

As Walter and I bike home, some of the guys pass us in their cars and trucks and honk their horns.

"Hey, Wally and Gibby. Race you!" Neko says, as he rolls up next to us in neutral, revving his engine. I swerve my bike so I don't get hit by one of his big side mirrors.

"I'll pick you guys up at 11:30," he says. "Be ready."

Then he peels away, kicking up dirt and dust with the back wheels of his truck. It's a good thing he's got mud flaps, or I'm sure I would've taken a rock to the head.

"I'm not going," I say to Walter as we turn into our neighborhood.

"You have to," he says. "I feel like this is my deal. You can't bail on me. Come on, man."

"Why did you even mention the farm?"

"I don't know. It just popped in my head. I'll text my cousin Eva and let her know we'll be heading out there tonight so she can distract my uncle if he hears any noise."

"Don't say anything to her!" I say. I don't need Walter's cousin getting me in trouble.

"She's cool," Walter says. I went to the farm a few years ago, and I don't remember her being "cool." She somehow tricked Walter and me into doing all of her chores while she sat up in the hayloft reading a book.

"I don't know," I say. "I have a bad feeling about this. Besides, our team should be focusing on getting ready for state, not on stealing cow poop."

"Cow manure," Walter corrects.

"Coach wasn't fooling around today. He was mad."

"Come on. What he doesn't know won't

hurt him." Before I could reply, Walter says, "I'll see you at 11:30. Don't wimp out on me."

"Fine!" I yell after him as he turns on his street. "But this is a really stupid idea."

Walter waves at me as he bikes away.

Chapter

9

I try to do my homework, but I fall asleep at my desk. At 11:30, I wake up to tapping at my window.

"Shhh." I hush Walter as I open the window.

I hear Gram shuffle down the hall.

"Toby, what's that sound?" she asks from just outside my door.

"I'm, umm, just studying," I tell Gram. "It was just me tapping my pencil. Sorry for waking you up. I'm going to bed now."

"Good night," she says, and I hear her go back to her room.

"Hurry up!" Walter hisses. "Neko is

getting antsy."

"I don't think I should leave," I whisper. "Gram is up. She might check on me again."

"Shove a pillow and some clothes under your covers. She'll never know you're gone," Walter says.

I roll my eyes and sigh. "Fine." Once I've done what he's suggested, I pull on a jacket, hat, and gloves. I'm not going to freeze again this time.

I slide out the window, grab a shovel from the tool shed, and run to the truck. I look back at Gram's window and I can't believe I'm doing this again. I'm so tired. I just want to crawl into my bed and pull the covers up, but Walter will never forgive me if I don't go, and he's always had my back.

When I get to the truck, I see Walter is sitting up front, between Neko and Cam. Jason is sitting in the back this time. I guess he's gotten on Neko's bad side.

I climb in beside Jason and pull my hat down over my ears as we head out of town.

Chapter 10

We're driving down a long gravel road a few miles outside of Edison. The farm is up ahead. I can see the dark outlines of the house and the barn. I also see a few cars and a minivan parked near the edge of a half-harvested cornfield.

Neko shuts the lights off on his truck, and we drive behind the barn. As I hop out, I can see a light go on upstairs in the house. I freeze. The light flicks off and back on again twice.

"It's just my cousin," Walter says, patting me on the shoulder. "She's letting us know my aunt and uncle are asleep."

He leads us through a metal gate to a huge

pile of manure next to the barn.

"You'll get used to the smell in a little bit,"
Walter says to the guys. I know this is true.
I've been here with Walter before, and after
a while, your nose adjusts. I fill up a bag with
cow poop, tie it up tightly, and hand it to one
of the bigger guys who hauls it to Neko's truck.

"Don't let any get in the bed of my truck,"
I hear Neko hiss. "Or you'll be scrubbing the
back of this thing until it's clean enough to
eat off of."

Behind me, a cow lets out a long, loud
bellow. I turn around and see three or four
cows slowly approaching us. Their eyes are
huge, and they're all staring at us.

"Walter," Jason says, slowly backing away.
"What do they want?"

"They won't hurt you," Walter says,
shaking open another bag. "They might lick
you, but they won't bite."

And sure enough, one of the cows moves
next to me, sticks out a slimy pink tongue, and
licks the back of my head.

"Go away," I hiss as I try to dump a huge

scoop of manure into the bag. As I try to dodge the cow's tongue I miss my target, and a big pile of cow poop lands on my shoe.

Soon, though, we've filled a dozen bags.

"Let's get out of here," Walter says, nervously looking back at the house. A light flicks on and off twice.

Instead of starting up the truck, Neko puts it in neutral, and we push it back across the road to where the other cars are parked.

Our teammates get back into their own vehicles. As cars start to pull out, Jason and I realize at the same time that we'll have to ride in the back of a truck filled with the cow poop. Jason jumps in a minivan, which drives away before I even have a chance to ask for a ride.

"I'm not sitting back there," I say to Walter, who's sitting inside the truck. "Move over. Make room."

"Get in the back," Neko says as Cam smirks at me and refuses to open the door.

"He can fit up here," Walter insists, trying to shift over on the seat.

"No, he can't," Neko says. "There's

no room."

Walter looks at me and I can see he's trapped. He's stuck in the middle of the truck between Cam and Neko. I sigh, but know it's no use arguing with Neko.

"I'll ride in the back," I say. "I'll be fine."

"You've got three seconds to get in, or I drive away," Neko warns.

I walk to the back of the truck. Just as I'm about to step on the bumper and climb in, Neko pulls away, and I lose my footing and fall on the gravel.

The sharp stones dig into my knees and hands.

The trucks keep driving, but then the brake lights go red, and Walter pushes his way out of the truck.

"Are you okay?" he says, running back to me.

"I'm fine." I try to stand up, but my jeans are ripped, and I can see my knee is bleeding.

Neko sticks his head out the window and looks back at us. "What did I tell you about being too slow?"

"He's hurt," Walter says.

"I'm fine," I say again, walking toward

the truck.

"Come on, baby," Neko taunts. "I'll get you back home to your mommy."

Now I'm mad. I don't like anybody talking about my mom. Especially Neko, who hasn't even bothered to get to know me enough to realize that my mom is in the military. That she's been deployed. I pick up a rock off the road and throw it hard at the back of his truck. It hits his taillight.

"Did you just throw a rock at my truck?" Neko shouts.

I throw another one, and it hits his back window.

"Find your own way home!" Neko yells back as he puts the truck in gear and speeds away.

"Idiots," Walter says as we stand there looking at the taillights disappear down the long dark road.

Chapter 11

Walter texts his cousin as we head back to the farm.

"Eva says she'll drive us home," Walter tells me as we wait behind a tree near the barn. "She just needs to a few minutes to sneak out."

I lean against a tree and shine the light from my phone down at my knee. The bleeding has stopped, and I realize the cut isn't that deep. I stand back up and press my back against the tree trunk, still fuming at Neko.

"Here she comes," Walter says, and we watch as his cousin sneaks out her window and climbs down the branches of a giant pine tree.

Once she drops to the ground, she makes her way toward us. Her curly, dark hair is piled into a messy bun on top of her head, and she's wearing a red hooded sweatshirt.

"Eva, do you remember Toby?" Walter asks.

Eva squints at me. "I think so," Eva says. "You came here once."

"Yeah," I say. "You made us do all your chores."

She laughs. "I don't remember that," she says as we walk toward an old station wagon parked near the barn.

"Sorry to make you drive us," I say.

She turns to Walter. "They just left you?"

"Yeah." Walter shrugs.

"Jerks," Eva mumbles. Then she notices my ripped jeans and bloody knee. "That doesn't look good." She bends down to look at the cut more closely.

"It isn't that deep. I'll be fine," I say. Walter tells her what happened.

"Make sure to wash it with soap and water when you get home," she says, straightening up and unlocking her car for us.

"Eva wants to be a nurse," Walter says as he climbs into the passenger seat and slams the door.

"Shh," Eva whispers. "You're going to wake up my dad."

"Sorry," he says.

We all freeze, watching the house for any signs of movement.

"I think we're good," Eva finally says.

Two minutes later she's driving us down the gravel road, away from the farm. "I want to be a doctor," she corrects Walter's previous comment. "But I might get my nursing degree first so I can understand everything from the front lines."

"Cool," I say.

"Toby's mom is an Army medic," Walter says. "Remember, I told you about her."

"Oh, right," Eva says. "Do you think I could talk to her? I was thinking of maybe taking that route."

"She's deployed right now," I say.

"How long?"

"She's probably got another five months."

"That's rough." I can hear the concern in Eva's voice, but she keeps her eyes on the road.

"Yeah," I say. "But they need her over there."

"I'd like to talk to her when she gets home, then," Eva says.

"Yeah, sure." I stare out the window as we merge onto the highway.

As we get near our exit, I notice that Eva doesn't put her blinker on.

"You need to exit here," I remind her.

"Since I'm driving you guys, I want to see what that team of yours is up to," she says, staying in her lane. "Let's drive by Winfield High and watch them spread the manure. I want to see them pinching their noses."

"Yeah," Walter agrees. "I want to watch them haul all those bags out on the field without our help."

I nod at this and say, "You know, they would've made the two of us do all the work."

We exit the highway and drive into Winfield, but when we get to the high school, no one is on the field.

Eva drives past the school. Neko's truck is

parked down by the locker room, but we don't see any sign of our teammates anywhere. Then the lights go on inside the building.

"What are they doing?" I ask.

"I think they just broke into the school," Eva says.

Four guys cross the road, and I realize one of them is Jason.

"Drive toward them," I tell Eva.

When we get near, Walter rolls the window down. "What's going on?"

"Neko and Cam and the rest of them are a bunch of idiots," Jason says. "What they're doing was never part of the plan. I'm out of here."

"What are they doing?" Walter asks.

"They're filling every player's locker with cow poop," Jason says, heading to a parked car with the three other guys.

"That's so wrong," Eva says from the front seat. "They're going to get caught. I'm sure there are security cameras recording their every move."

If that's true, I don't want to be anywhere

near the school. "Let's get out of here," I say.

Walter rolls up his window and slides down in his seat as we slowly drive out of Winfield.

Chapter 12

We cross over into Edison and I start to feel a little safer, being in my hometown. But just then, as we pass the high school, a car peels out of our school parking lot and zooms past us. A red BMW. The same one Walter and I frosted just a few days ago. Two other cars follow.

"What are they up to?" Walter wonders out loud.

"Nothing good," Eva says.

"Drive by so we can get a closer look," Walter says.

"No way," Eva retorts. "I'm bringing you guys home. There's way too much stupidity going down tonight."

Eva drops me off first.

"Thanks," I say. "We'd still be walking if it wasn't for you."

"Don't worry about it. Hey, can I have your number? I really *would* like to talk to your mom when she gets back."

"Sure," I say, and we exchange numbers.

"And uh . . ." Eva looks away from me, like she's suddenly embarrassed. "Let me know how this all turns out."

"I will," I say. She smiles at me as she pulls away, and I head across the lawn and to the side of my house.

Just as I'm about to climb back in my window, I remember my manure-covered shoes, which I slip off and leave outside. I'll have to hose them down in the morning. There's no way I can bring them into the house.

Back in my room, I realize my clothes reek too. I take them off, spray them with some body spray, and shove them under my bed beside the clothes that have frosting all over them. I'm going to have to do a full load of secret laundry when Gram's not home. I'm down to one clean pair of jeans.

Just as I'm about to drift off to sleep, the phone in the kitchen rings. Two rings. Three rings. And then I hear Gram answer. My heart feels like it has stopped beating, and I'm suddenly having a hard time breathing. I know that a call this late at night never brings good news. Something must have happened to my mom.

Chapter 13

Gram knocks on my door and enters my room with the kitchen phone in her hand.

"Your coach wants to talk to you."

I'm instantly relieved that it isn't bad news about my mom, but that relief doesn't last long. Now I'm scared to know why Coach is calling me this late at home.

I sit up in my bed and pretend I've been asleep for hours.

"Hello," I say into the phone in a sleepy voice.

"Toby?"

"Yeah, Coach?"

"You're at home? In bed?"

"Ahh, yeah," I say, looking at my Gram standing in the doorway.

"Good," he says. "That's where you should be. Now get some sleep."

He hangs up the phone.

Gram sits down on the end of my bed and takes the phone from me.

"Sounds like some of your teammates got into trouble tonight," she says to me. "Do you know what they were up to?"

I shake my head.

She brushes the hair away from my forehead. And then she wrinkles her nose. "Why do you smell like the inside of a barn?"

Chapter 14

I tell Gram everything. I've felt so guilty lying to her these past few days, and it doesn't seem worth it anymore. She'll find out what happened soon enough, so I might as well let her know now.

"You need to call your coach back," she says. "Tell him what you just told me. It's better to tell the truth and take the punishment right away than to let it simmer for too long and get worse."

She gestures to my cell phone and leaves the room, but instead of calling Coach, I text Walter.

Me: *You up?*

Him: *Yeah.*

Me: *Did you talk to Coach?*

Him: *Yeah. Good thing we were home and in bed. Did you hear what happened?*

Me: *No.*

Him: *Neko, Cam, and six other seniors were caught breaking into the locker room. They set off some alarm, and the police came. They all got hauled down to the police station.*

Me: *What's going to happen to them?*

Him: *It won't be good.*

We agree to meet in the morning, and I crawl farther under the covers of my bed. I know I should call Coach, but I also know that he's probably dealing with a lot right now. So I decide that I'll talk to him in the morning. Besides, my mom has always told me it's better to talk to someone face-to-face.

I try to fall asleep, but I toss and turn. I hear Gram get up at five, but I just lie in bed wide awake, wondering what will happen to me when I tell Coach I was part of this whole thing.

Chapter 15

Walter and I walk slowly to school in the morning. I told him what Gram said and have convinced him to turn himself in with me. We're both nervous. Walter isn't even snacking on anything. We don't know what will happen to the guys who were caught, and we don't know what will happen to us.

As we make our way through the parking lot at school, we see what the Wildcats were up to. In front of our school, a dumpster has been tipped over. Beneath the pile of garbage are the words TRASH EDISON, spray-painted in huge blaze orange letters on the sidewalk.

"That's not even the worst part," one of the guys from our team says, coming up to us. "Check out what they did to our field."

We walk to the chain-link fence that surrounds our field, and I see big patches of dead grass. It looks like the Winfield guys poured some sort of weed or grass killer in the shape of a W on it last night. The grass is yellow and shriveled. We see Coach and our principal standing out there.

"We should talk to him." I turn to Walter.

"Not now," Walter says, and I know he's right. Even from this far away, I can see that Coach is more upset than I've seen him before. He's pacing back and forth. He's kicking at the grass, and the principal shakes her head.

Walter checks his phone as we head to class.

"They've been suspended," he says.

"Who?" I ask.

"Neko, Cam, and the others."

"From school?"

"Not just that," Walter says. "From our team. They aren't going to state. The only two seniors left are Zander and Jason."

"What?" I say, shocked. "We've lost almost all of our good starters. How are we going to even play?"

I look over at the spray-painted sidewalk in front of our school and get even angrier.

"What about the Wildcats?" I ask as we walk into the building. "What about what they did? Did any of those guys get caught and punished?"

"I haven't heard anything. I have a feeling they got away with it."

It turns out that pretty much the whole school has heard about what happened—and a lot of people are angry at our team. We just threw away our chances at winning state. Those of us who weren't involved with the break-in, who aren't suspended, still get plenty of glares in the hall.

"What were you guys thinking?" people ask again and again. Even my teachers seem disappointed in me. And I can't act like I had nothing to do with any of it because I did. If it hadn't been for Neko's stupid comment about my mom, I might have been at Winfield High and gotten suspended too. I'd like to think I would have walked away with Jason and the others, but I'm not so sure I would have been able to.

***

When the bell rings for lunch, I convince Walter that we should go down to Coach's office. I don't want to walk into the cafeteria anyway. I don't want to feel all those eyes. I feel like our team has betrayed our school.

My stomach is in knots as we walk to Coach's office.

I take a deep breath and knock on the door.

"Come in!" he shouts.

Coach is sitting at his desk. He's scrolling through news articles on his computer. He looks exhausted and hurt. We've had such a great season. A winning season. He's been so proud of this team, and now we've let him down.

"Boys," he says, not looking up.

"We wanted to talk," I say, trying to keep my voice calm and even.

He points to two chairs in front of his desk.

"Talk," he says, looking at the two of us.

"I wanted to tell you that I was in on the prank," I say.

"But we never went to Winfield High," Walter interrupts. "We weren't there for that part. We didn't know they were going to break into the school. The original plan was just to go on the field."

"We filled bags with cow poop," I say. "The plan was just to spread it on the field. That was all."

"I know you two weren't there," Coach says. "There's video."

"We just wanted to say we're sorry," I say. "Really sorry. We should've stopped the whole thing, but we didn't."

Coach doesn't say anything. His silence is worse than yelling. He just stares at his computer screen.

Walter and I look at each other, not sure if we should stand up and leave or just sit there.

Finally Coach says, "You two are the only ones who've come in to speak to me today."

Walter and I both look down at the floor.

"I'm not happy that you were part of this," Coach continues, "but I'm glad you and some of the other guys were smart enough to walk away."

Coach stands up and moves to a window that overlooks the football field.

"You two are going to have to work harder than you've ever worked before. You'll be starting at state. We've lost our top players, so you and the rest of the team are going to have to step up. And because you two were the first ones with enough guts to talk to me face to face, you'll be my team captains for the next few days."

Walter looks at me. I'm not sure what to say, so I just do what Gram told me to do when someone gives me something—stand up, stretch out your hand, and say, "Thank you."

Coach shakes my hand.

Walter stands up and sticks out his hand too.

I leave Coach's office feeling as if we're in over our heads. There wasn't a lot of pressure just sitting on the bench. The winning wasn't really up to us. We spent most of the year in the background, but now we're both going to play at state. We're going to have to lead. We're going to have to try to get this team back on our feet after losing most of our top players— our biggest and best.

"I don't know how we're going to do this," Walter says as we head back to class.

"I don't either," I agree. "But we don't have a choice."

"Do you think Neko will murder us in our sleep?" Walter asks. I think he's only half joking.

"I don't think he cares about us right now," I say as we stop at my locker and I take out some books. "He's been kicked off the team. He's not going to state. He might even end up in jail."

Chapter 16

Practice is tough. It feels like we just buried half our team, and as if losing our star players wasn't bad enough, we have to run plays across the chemically scarred grass. Nobody is focused on practice or even state anymore.

Everyone keeps asking, "How are we going to do this? How are we going to win?"

Coach doesn't even give us a pep talk. He's too busy moving players to new positions, trying to come up with a new plan.

"Get them focused," Coach tells Walter and me before practice. "Get them running plays."

Walter and I try, but it isn't happening. No

one is even trying. The whole practice is a big fat mess.

I call everyone together at the end of practice. "Team dinner. My house. Seven. Everyone be there," I say with as much authority as I can manage.

I've decided that if there is one thing this team needs, it's a good meal. And maybe that will change everyone's attitude. Gram always feeds people when things are bad, so I've decided I'll use the same strategy.

Coach catches my eye and nods. I guess he approves.

I rush home to warn Gram that I've just invited the entire team over. Before I even finish my sentence, she's opening cupboards and pulling out pans. She sends me into the basement to haul up some of her canned tomatoes and dried basil. Then she has me set up our giant card table and folding chairs in the garage.

I'm not totally sure anyone will show up. Most of the upperclassmen are used to ignoring me. What if I've made Gram do all this work for nothing?

But at seven the whole team arrives, including Coach. Everyone is quiet at first, but by the end of dinner, even Coach is smiling. The energy in the room is so much different than it was at practice earlier. *We might just be okay*, I think to myself.

Everyone thanks Gram when they leave, and she gives everyone a hug. It's a funny scene, all these big guys in Gram's skinny arms.

When it's Coach's turn he adds, "I've missed your cooking. The school cafeteria isn't the same without it. Thank you for feeding us all tonight."

"Oh, this?" she says. "This is something I just whipped up. Imagine what I'll feed you all if you win state."

***

The next day at practice, we slowly get it together. Play by play, we build up our confidence. Walter is faster than he was just a few months ago, and his height is an advantage. He's able to pick balls out of the air.

Halfway through practice, I see Neko's truck parked next to a road overlooking the field. He and a few guys are watching us. It makes me nervous, and I mess up two plays. Coach calls me over.

"You know this," he tells me. "You can run these plays. You're ready for this. Just have confidence in yourself."

I'm rattled by Neko and the others watching, but I don't tell Coach. I'm hoping they'll just go away, and sure enough, in a few minutes, they're gone.

After practice, while Walter and I are walking home, we know before we turn around that Neko's truck is right behind us. We know the sound of the engine, the tires, the music he plays.

Neko pulls up beside us. "Get in."

Chapter 17

"**G**otta get home," Walter says. "I can't be late."

"Get in," Neko says again. "You two have some work to do."

I look at Walter and nod. I don't think Neko is out to get us, but I'm not totally sure. I do know that I want him to see that I'm not afraid of him. I walk around the truck and open the passenger door. Walter follows, and we both climb in.

Neko drives to the edge of town—to the empty field where we met to plan our first prank.

"Get out," he says.

We slide out and he gets out too. A minute later, Cam and some of the other guys show up.

"So you two are the new team captains?" Neko asks, looking us up and down.

"Kind of," Walter replies.

"Are you or aren't you?" Neko asks again.

"Yes," I say. "For now."

"Then you've got to be ready."

He grabs a bag of footballs and some orange cones out of the back his trunk, and we follow him down to the field.

For an hour, Neko and the other guys coach us.

"You have to be faster," Neko shouts when I step back to throw the ball. "The Wildcats aren't just fast, they're mean. They'll get in your face. They'll try to rattle you. They'll send their biggest linemen to crush you like a grape. So whatever you do, keep your eyes up, and don't ever stop moving your feet."

We set up a formation. Cam snaps the ball, and Neko and two other linemen descend on me before I can even look for a receiver.

They don't hit me hard, but they push me

to let me know they got to me.

"Faster," Neko says, and we run the play again.

After a dozen times, I finally get faster and more accurate when forced to throw under pressure, and Walter gets better at knowing where to expect the ball.

"Coach is going to want you to call a lot of lateral passes," Neko tells me. "But I'm sure the Wildcats are going to expect it too, so you're going to have to use that arm of yours and throw the ball long. You've got a good, tall friend who can catch whatever you throw. You two are a team. You've got this."

We practice for an hour and agree to meet again the next day.

As Neko drives us back to our neighborhood, I ask about the Wildcats and about the guys who ruined our field and spray-painted the sidewalk in front of our school.

"The school's security cameras weren't working. I guess they haven't worked for months. Too expensive to repair. So they have no evidence and no way of proving which guys vandalized our school."

"We saw Lars's BMW drive out of the parking lot," Walter says.

"Yeah," Neko says. "That doesn't matter. No one is going to believe you. You're an Eddie with a grudge."

Neko drops off Walter and then pulls into my driveway. I see Gram at the window. She's probably wondering where I've been.

"Do you want to come inside?" I say. "On Thursdays my Gram makes this incredible bread."

Neko sits there for a moment.

"Come in," I say. "Just for a slice."

"Sure," Neko finally says. "What else do I have to do?"

Inside, I introduce Neko to Gram. "He's been helping me get ready for state," I tell her.

Neko looks embarrassed. "Least I can do," he mumbles. "I'm the reason you're carrying all this pressure." I'm sure Gram knows he's one of the guys who got suspended, but she doesn't treat him any differently than she treats Walter. She just has us sit down in the kitchen and cuts each of us a huge slice of bread.

He takes a bite, and a broad smile forms across his face.

Gram pours herself a cup of tea and walks back to her room, leaving us alone.

"I messed up," Neko whispers when we're alone in the kitchen.

I study him. He doesn't seem to look as big anymore. He used to stand up tall like he owned the place wherever he went, but now he shuffles along, head down, from place to place. It's like he was a balloon and someone let all of the air out of him.

"Yeah, you did. But it doesn't have to be the end for you," I say. " Maybe what you need to do now to get past this is apologize. Apologize, fix what you can, and things will work themselves out."

"Yeah," Neko says, looking at me. "I don't know."

"I do," I say. "You made a mistake. Just admit it. What do you have to lose?"

Chapter 18

On Friday we make the near-silent bus ride to state. It's less than an hour to the city, but the ride seems to take forever. There's an emptiness without Neko and Cam and the other guys on board. The usual energy on the bus before a game is gone. No one is joking around. All of us are lost in our own thoughts.

Yesterday Neko apologized to Coach and to our team. Then he wrote a letter of apology and submitted it to the school newspaper—*and* the Winfield newspaper. It hasn't run the papers yet, but it's already spread all over social media. He talked about making amends for what he and the other guys had done.

Instead of going to state, Neko, Cam, and the rest of the guys are spending the weekend scrubbing down the Wildcats' locker room and repainting each and every locker with a fresh coat of paint, then digging up the dead grass and repairing our football field. It's good to know that whatever happens at state, we'll all have a fresh start next season.

***

As we head through the crowd to our locker room, I see Eva waving to me.

"You never texted me," she shouts over the heads of the crowd.

"It's been a crazy week," I yell back.

"But it's all going to turn out all right," she says, smiling.

"I hope so," I reply.

"Text me," she says as she walks back to the crowd.

I take out my phone and send her a message.

Thanks for being here, I write and push send.

I see her stop and turn around.

I wouldn't miss it for the world, she texts back. *Good luck. Don't give up.*

I beam at my phone.

"What's up with you and my cousin?" Walter asks, coming up to me.

"I don't know," I say. "But I do know that I like her more than I did when I met her three years ago."

Walter smiles at this and says to me, "Just know, she will always be smarter than you."

I nod at this. "I don't doubt it."

Chapter
19

While we're changing in the locker room, there's a knock on the door.

Coach disappears outside and then comes back in and tells me to get dressed and come out in the hall with him.

Just outside the locker room door, Gram is waiting for me, holding a grocery bag in one hand and her phone in the other.

"Your mother is on the line," she says. "She's back to base safe and sound, and she wants to talk to you."

There is static and my mom's faraway voice.

"Toby," she says. "I'm so proud of you. So

much has happened since we talked last."

"Yeah, it has," I say. I don't know how much Gram has told her, and I figure there isn't time to explain everything right now.

"I just want you to know you can do this. I'm proud of you," she says.

"I'm proud of you too," I reply.

"My unit is going to watch your game. Your grandmother is going to feed it to us live over the internet. I just want you to know we are all rooting for you over here."

"I'll do my best," I say.

"I know you will," my mom says before we get disconnected.

I hand the phone back to Gram. She gives me a hug and hands me the grocery bag, which is full of snacks for the team: giant containers of apple slices, orange wedges, and oatmeal chocolate chip cookies.

Back in the locker room, Coach nods at me and I pass around the container of cookies.

"You've got this, boys," Coach says. "The Wildcats have never played half of you before. There is no film for them to study. So all you need to do is surprise them again and again. They have no idea how focused and determined and strong you are."

So that's our plan for the game—do the unexpected. Keep the Wildcats on their toes.

"Go Eddies!" Walter shouts and then takes a huge bite of his cookie. We all do the same. We head onto the field with cookie crumbs on our jerseys.

Chapter 20

We decide to go big. Our third play of the game, we give the Wildcats the surprise of their lives. We run a flea-flicker.

I hand the ball to Jason, who runs a sweep and then passes the ball back to a new freshman lineman who reverses back to me. As he pitches me the ball I spot Walter open near the sideline. I throw a long pass and Walter catches it. With no one in front of him, he runs in for an easy touchdown. No one expected it. The crowd goes crazy. The kick is good, and the Wildcats stand on the field trying to figure out what just happened. We're ahead 7–0.

The Wildcats thought this was going to be an easy win with Neko and some of our biggest players gone, but everyone on our team is stepping up and ready to win.

At the end of the first quarter, the Wildcats throw a pass into the end zone, but Zander, who is now playing safety, leaps up, deflects the balls, and then picks it off and runs it all the way to the fifty yard line. Interception! We gain possession of the ball. I make a pass to Walter. He catches it again. Touchdown!

"You've got them rattled," Coach says to us on the sideline. "Keep it up."

And we do. Until the start of the second quarter, when I throw an interception and the Wildcats run it in for a touchdown. They score again with just three seconds left of the first half. We're tied 14–14.

Chapter 21

At halftime, I pick at an orange wedge and try to stay calm. I feel really bad about the interception, but Coach tells me I have to shake it off.

"We're going to keep throwing the ball," Coach tells us. "The Wildcats are too big to run against, so Gibson needs to keep making deep passes. And receivers, you need to be prepared to catch everything. No interceptions."

The pressure is on me to make sure I throw fast and on target.

When we head out to the field for the

third quarter, the Wildcats stick to Walter like gum. He can't get open. And we can't get a first down.

When the Wildcats get possession, they find their groove and march the ball down the field. They get first down after first down, and in five plays they push right through our line and get another touchdown.

Their fans are on their feet, stomping in the stands, and I see them hold up signs mocking us.

One of the signs says, "*Trash the Eddies!*" There are photographs of Neko and Cam with garbage taped next to them.

This makes me mad. They've got players on their team who broke the law too—who dumped trash all over our school and scarred our field—but all of them are playing now.

When we huddle up, I tell Walter I'm going to try another pass to him, but I can tell Jason is afraid the pass will be intercepted again.

"Just everyone get open," I say.

We line up.

The ball is snapped.

I step back, but the Wildcats break through our offensive line. I run backward and then fake out a huge defender, cut up a hole I see in the middle of the field, and run down the field as if I'm being chased by Lars Bristol's giant dog.

I see Jason next to me, and I throw a lateral pass to him just before I get tackled.

Bam! I'm flat on the field.

For a moment, I lose my breath, but then I hear the cheering from the stands.

Jason has run the ball in for a touchdown.

The play was a mess, but we did what we had to do.

I look over at Coach and I can see he's signaling for us to fake the kick and go for a two-point conversion.

He sends out the special teams.

It looks like we're going to kick the extra point, but when the ball is snapped, the holder throws it to Zander and he runs into the end zone.

We are ahead by one point.

Chapter
22

During the fourth quarter, the Wildcats start marching down the field again, but we stop them in their tracks. Zander manages to knock the ball out of a Winfield receiver's hands. It bounces around on the field. One of our players pounces on it, and it's ours again.

Coach calls a timeout and I run over to the sideline. "Don't pass," Coach tells me. "We have to run the ball and run the clock out."

"I don't know," I say. "The Wildcats' defense is a wall. I don't know if we'll even get a first down."

"We can't risk a pick," Coach says.

I nod at this, and we take the field.

The Wildcats are prepared for us to run.

I hand the ball off to Jason, but he only makes it three yards before he's taken down. We try the play again, but he gets tackled for a loss. We're losing ground.

I look over at Coach. We can't let the Wildcats get the ball. He signals for me to throw.

For the next play, I pretend to hand the ball off to Jason, faking the Wildcats' defenders out. It buys me just enough time to spot Walter near the sideline. I throw the ball high over the other players' heads and Walter has to leap to catch it, but he does. He could easily just step out of bounds and get us a first down, but instead, he runs down the sideline as if he is on a balance beam. The Wildcats chase after him, but Walter's legs are long, and he is faster than any Wildcats' defender. He breaks away from everyone and scores a touchdown.

Chapter 23

On Saturday we celebrate our new state title
at the school. Gram gets the cafeteria kitchen
back for the day. She and some of her old
coworkers cook up a storm. I invite Eva to
come as my date.

When we enter the cafeteria, it has been
transformed. Parents and some of the kids
from school have spent the day decorating the
place. There are tablecloths on every table and
a hundred balloons. Someone even donated
speakers and a sound system.

Before the meal, Coach gives a short speech
and has all the players stand up, including Neko,

Cam, and the other players who were suspended from the team. He gives them a shout-out for their hard work. They not only painted lockers and restored our field, but they've spent the last few days painting and cleaning up the park across the street from our school.

As the event winds down, Gram gets on the microphone and promises leftovers to anyone who helps clean up. Half the school ends up staying. In less than an hour the cafeteria is spotless, and everyone has an extra plate loaded up with food.

As Gram and I are about to leave, the principal comes up to us. "Mrs. Gibson," she says to Gram, "We all miss your amazing food. I know you're enjoying your retirement, but I wonder if you'd be willing to make some food for our concession stand. I think we could make a fortune off those cookies you bake."

Gram smiles all the way home.

"Thank you," I tell her as we walk into the house. "You've been amazing. I just wish Mom could've been here."

"Next year," Gram says. "All you have to do

is make it to state again, and you know what? I think you all can do it. I just need to feed that team of yours and put some meat on some of those bony guys." I can tell Gram is already putting recipes together in her head.

I hug her and kiss the top of her fuzzy head.

As I head to my room, my phone buzzes and I see that it's Eva texting me.

Good night, she writes.

Good night at the end of a good day, I write back. I'm looking forward to talking to her more. But for now, I'm ready to finally get some sleep.

Check out all the titles in the

bOunCe

Collection

STEP UP YOUR GAME

About the Author

K. R. Coleman is a writer, teacher, and parent of two boys. Coleman can often be found jotting down ideas in a notebook while watching a hockey or baseball game or while walking along the many trails that encircle Minneapolis. Currently, Coleman teaches at the Loft Literary Center and is working on a young adult novel entitled *Air*.